Sinbad

Legend Of The Seven Seas

SINBAD and MARINA

adapted by Cathy Hapka

DREAMWORKS®

PUFFIN BOOKS
Published by Penguin Group
Penguin Young Readers Group,
345 Hudson Street, New York, New York 10014, U.S.A.
Penguin Books Ltd, 80 Strand, London WC2R ORL, England
Penguin Books Australia Ltd, Ringwood, Victoria, Australia
Penguin Books Canada Ltd, 10 Alcorn Avenue, Toronto, Ontario, Canada M4V 3B2
Penguin Books (N.Z.) Ltd, 182-190 Wairau Road, Auckland 10, New Zealand

Published by Puffin Books, a division of Penguin Young Readers Group, 2003

1 3 5 7 9 10 8 6 4 2

Sinbad: Legend of the Seven Seas TM & © 2003 DreamWorks, L.L.C.
All rights reserved

ISBN 0-14-250105-0

Printed in the United States of America

CONTENTS

CHAPTER ONE
The Book of Peace

The city of Syracuse sparkled in the moonlight. The towers and temples gleamed and the broad, clean streets were quiet. In the harbor, grand ships bobbed side by side, and sailors cheerfully went about their work.

Overlooking it all stood the palace of King Dymas. The palace was always an impressive sight, but tonight the golden light of hundreds of lanterns made it look more glorious than ever. Music and laughter poured into the night from within its walls, cloaking the city with joy.

The Delegation of the Twelve Cities had arrived earlier that day at the invitation of the king. Everyone wanted to be a part of the celebration now that the fabled Book of Peace had come to Syracuse at last. The Book protected the Twelve Cities, and would stay in Syracuse for 100 years. Then it would move on to another city.

Inside the palace, a beautiful, dark-haired young ambassador named Marina was enjoying the party. She sometimes grew bored with palace parties, but this was a truly special occasion.

"Here she is," she heard from behind her. She immediately

recognized the voice of the king's son, Proteus. "I've told her all about you. Sinbad, I would like to introduce you to my fiancée, the Lady Marina, Ambassador from Thrace."

Marina was surprised. Sinbad? Had she heard the prince right?

She turned and saw a handsome, bearded young man standing beside Proteus. The stranger wasn't dressed for the formal occasion. But there was a gleam in his eyes that captured her interest right away.

"So this is the infamous Sinbad," Marina said lightly. "I heard all about you this morning. First you try to rob Proteus, then you save his life. So which are you, a thief or a hero?"

She already knew the answer. Proteus, the king's only son, had been sailing toward Syracuse with the Book when a shipload of pirates had tried to steal it. Sinbad, Proteus's childhood best friend, was their leader.

While they were fighting over the Book, a sea monster—sent by Eris, the Goddess of Chaos—had attacked both ships. Sinbad had risked his own life to save Proteus—at least that was how Proteus had described it to Marina. Of course, she knew that the prince always saw only the best in people. Marina found it one of his most appealing attributes—even if it sometimes made him a little too trusting for his own good.

Proteus smiled uncertainly at Marina. "Sinbad wanted to give me an opportunity to thank him …"

His voice trailed off as he glanced at the spot where Sinbad had been standing a second ago. But the uninvited guest had disappeared just as quickly as he had arrived.

The couple soon spotted Sinbad and his men leaving the ballroom. What was going on? By the time Proteus and Marina pushed their way through the crowds and reached the door, Sinbad was long gone.

The couple decided to step out into the palace gardens for a breath of fresh air. It was a beautiful night. The light from the Book Tower sparkled and danced across the water.

"Look at it this way," Marina said with a laugh. "Now that Sinbad's gone, your father can relax and enjoy the evening."

She knew the king couldn't be happy about having a thief as a guest on such an important night.

Proteus smiled in return. "You're right about that," he agreed. "He's trying not to show it, but he's so proud to have the Book in Syracuse. He's been planning this day his whole life."

By now they had reached a balcony overlooking the sea. "Soon it'll be your responsibility," Marina commented.

"*Our* responsibility," Proteus corrected with a smile.

Marina smiled back, then stared out toward the moonlit water for a moment. "It's beautiful," she said.

"It is," Proteus agreed eagerly, glancing up at the impressive Book Tower rising behind them. He was still thinking about the Book of Peace. "There are guards on every level and if you look up to—"

Noticing Marina's smile, he stopped in mid-sentence and grinned sheepishly.

"You were talking about the ocean, weren't you?" he said.

She returned her gaze to the sea. "I only wish I'd seen more of it. I used to imagine sailing far beyond the Twelve Cities and discovering the world."

"Marina," Proteus said seriously, "our marriage was arranged many years ago. But politics is not a reason to get married—I don't want you to do this just because it's your duty."

Before they could finish the discussion, King Dymas rushed up to them. "There you are!" he cried breathlessly to Marina. "I think the delegates from Manoli are trying to give a toast—although I'm not sure." He shrugged helplessly. "They're doing something with their knees..."

Marina glanced at Proteus, then smiled at the king. "Of course, Sire," she said, taking his arm. Ever since she was a little girl, Marina had loved to learn about exotic lands and different cultures. Even though she didn't travel much now, the king still counted on her to help him understand the language and behavior of visitors who came to the city from faraway lands.

It wasn't the same as seeing those lands for herself. But her life was in Syracuse now, not on the open sea.

Of course, that didn't mean she couldn't still dream of what might have been.

CHAPTER TWO
Stolen!

Back in the ballroom, the enormous chandelier overhead suddenly began to rattle. The ground shook. The huge domed ceiling shuddered, and cracks formed on its smooth surface.

People screamed and ran in terror. The palace guards grabbed the king and pulled him away to safety. What was happening? Was it an earthquake?

Proteus took Marina's hand. Together, they raced outside.

The rumble was just as loud out there. All around them, the pair could hear the creak and groan of buildings shaking on their foundations.

Marina looked up at the Book Tower. A dark cloud poured out of it, thicker and blacker than any smoke she'd ever seen. It oozed out over the city, blanketing it like a bad dream.

"Proteus!" Marina cried. "The Book!"

Proteus nodded. His face grim, he rushed toward the Tower.

An hour later, the city was in chaos. The Book was gone. Everyone was sure who had taken it—Sinbad. His dagger had been found at the scene of the crime. The king's guards caught him on his ship. They brought him back to the palace, and threw him in prison.

Proteus went to see his old friend in his cell. But Sinbad denied the charges, insisting upon his own innocence. He claimed he had been framed by Eris, the Goddess of Chaos.

The guards brought their prisoner into the throne room in chains. King Dymas frowned at Sinbad as the delegates from the Twelve Cities sat in judgment.

"We've heard enough of your lies," the king said sternly. "Sinbad, for the last time, give us the Book!"

"How many times do I have to say it?" Sinbad retorted. "I don't have it!"

Marina winced as she watched the proceedings. King Dymas was a merciful man—if Sinbad would only confess, surely he would be allowed to live. Why was he so stubborn?

"Very well then," the head ambassador spoke grimly. "The

Delegation of the Twelve Cities finds you guilty of treason—and we sentence you to die." He glared at Sinbad. "Take him away."

Sinbad struggled as the guards dragged him toward the door. "Come on," he pleaded. "This is a joke, right? You're making a mistake. Are you people blind? I didn't do it!"

"Stop!"

Was that Proteus? Marina stood up in surprise, trying to get a better look.

The prince strode forward through the crowd. Murmurs rose on every side as Proteus stopped at Sinbad's side. As King Dymas stepped forward, Proteus looked straight at him.

"I demand the right of substitution," the prince declared. "Take me in his place."

Marina gasped along with the rest of the crowd. The right of substitution! How could he make such a choice? How could he offer to die in place of the real thief?

"No!" King Dymas cried out in horror.

Proteus glanced at Sinbad, who looked just as surprised as everyone else. "Sinbad says that Eris took the Book," Proteus said. "And I believe him. Let him go to Tartarus and recover it."

"What?" Sinbad gasped. He grabbed at Proteus. "Hey, look—I will not be responsible for your life!"

"You would do the same for me," Proteus replied.

Sinbad shook his head. "No," he said. "I wouldn't."

King Dymas reached toward his son. "If Sinbad is allowed to leave the city, he'll never come back!" he exclaimed. "Son, listen to reason."

"No, Father, you listen," Proteus said. "Sinbad either stole the Book, or he's telling the truth and it's in Tartarus. Either way, he's our only hope."

Despite her own horror and surprise, Marina had to admire the logic of Proteus's argument. It was true. Sinbad might be the only one who could return the Book to Syracuse. He would have to follow Eris's star beyond the horizon to get to Tartarus.

The head ambassador spoke again. "Proteus," he said solemnly, "you realize that if Sinbad does not return, you will be put to death in his place."

Proteus nodded. "I understand."

"So be it," the ambassador said. "Sinbad has ten days to return the Book."

King Dymas was beside himself with shock and grief. But he pulled himself together and turned to the guards holding Sinbad.

"Release him," the king said, his voice steady.

As the guards removed the pirate's chains, Marina glared at Sinbad. How could he do this? He and Proteus were friends. She was still convinced that Sinbad had taken the Book himself.

The guards took hold of Proteus. As they started to lead him away, the prince turned. "Oh, and Sinbad," he said. "Don't be late."

With one last furious glance at Sinbad, Marina followed as the guards led Proteus out of the room.

CHAPTER THREE
A Stowaway on the *Chimera*

A few hours before dawn, Marina slipped out of the palace and made for the harbor. She didn't want anyone to see her leave. It was clear what she had to do. She didn't want to waste time arguing with anyone who thought her plan was too risky. She just hoped she wasn't too late.

By the soft light of the stars, she soon spotted Sinbad's ship, the *Chimera*, bobbing gently on the waves. She smiled, and a shiver of nervousness ran through her. With a quick glance to make sure no one was around, she headed for the gangplank.

It didn't take much for Marina to bribe her way onto the ship, just a few jewels she had brought for that very purpose. She stayed out of sight below deck until she felt the ship moving off. Muffled shouts drifted down from above. After waiting a few more minutes, she crept up to the deck.

It was still dark, but a lantern burned on deck. Sinbad was standing there with his first mate, Kale, a huge man with a shiny bald head. Marina tiptoed as close as she dared, staying hidden as she listened to them speak.

"So," Kale said, "any idea how we actually get to Tartarus?"

Sinbad turned to look at him. "Tartarus?" he repeated. "People get killed in Tartarus!"

"So where are we going?" Kale sounded surprised.

"Fiji!" Sinbad declared.

Marina clenched her fists. She had been right. Sinbad had no intention of trying to save Proteus!

Not needing to hear any more, she backed away, heading toward Sinbad's cabin. She might as well check to see if the Book of Peace was on the ship.

A quick search of Sinbad's cabin turned up no sign of the Book. But there were all sorts of other artifacts and treasures there. Marina was amazed at the variety. How many exotic places had Sinbad visited in his travels? How many wondrous things had he seen, or taken?

"Stolen from Venezia," she murmured, examining a dagger. "From Pompeii," she added, noticing a metal amulet.

"Good guess," a voice said behind her.

Marina spun around, startled. She had been so distracted by the treasures that she hadn't heard Sinbad enter.

"What do you think you're doing here?" he demanded.

Marina quickly regained her composure. Sinbad was a tough and experienced sailor, but she wasn't going to let him see that he made her a little nervous.

"I'm here to make sure you get the Book of Peace." She shrugged. "Sinbad, you're not a very complicated guy. All someone has to do is imagine the most gutless course of action and you're bound to take it."

"Hey, this is not my problem." Sinbad sounded defensive. "I didn't steal the Book." He plopped down on his bunk.

This time, Marina actually believed him. But she thought

of Proteus sitting in the cell meant for Sinbad. He trusted his old friend to do the right thing.

"You're really not going to lose any sleep over this, are you?" she asked.

"Not a wink," he replied immediately.

She shrugged again. "Because, me, I'd be tossing and turning, knowing I'm alive because I let my friend die."

It was obvious that the words hit him hard. He sat up straight, his expression twisting into one of irritation and guilt.

"I'm not responsible for this mess." Sinbad jumped out of the bunk. "I didn't ask Proteus to put his neck on the line for me."

"Clearly I can't appeal to your 'honor,'" Marina told him. "But I have other ways of convincing you."

"Oh, really." He sounded skeptical. "Just how do you expect to do that?"

"By speaking your language." Turning to face him, she revealed a large, glittering gem. As she held it up, it caught the light and sparkled brightly. Marina saw Sinbad's eyes widen slightly, but he quickly hid his reaction.

"Keep talking," he said.

She pulled out a velvet bag and dumped two more beautiful jewels into Sinbad's hand. Then she stepped back and waited for his response. She pasted a confident smile on her face, trying not to look as nervous as she felt.

"Hmm." Sinbad studied the gems. "This'll do . . ."

Marina's smile broadened. It had worked!

" . . . but not for first class."

Her smile faded.

The Dragon's Teeth

"I 'd like to introduce you to your new bunkmate," Sinbad announced, stepping into a cramped storage room. Marina was slung over his shoulder like a sack of potatoes. No matter how hard she fought, she couldn't break free of his strong grip. "Well, actually you're his new bunkmate," he said as he lowered her to the floor. "It's his bunk."

Marina stared at the ship's dog, Spike. He was a large, funny-looking dog, with small ears, a big nose, and a slimy stream of drool hanging off his lower lip. But his odd looks were nothing compared to his very odd smell. It was like a combination of stale dog biscuits and rotten eggs. The dog climbed into Marina's lap and licked her face as Sinbad stepped out and locked the door behind him.

Marina groaned, pushing Spike away. Her new quarters weren't exactly luxurious. But as long as Sinbad kept his word to change course for Tartarus, she could live with it. If she didn't breathe in too deeply.

But she couldn't live with being a prisoner. Absentmindedly, she took a ribbon from her pouch and wrapped it around her

hand. Marina didn't want to miss the most exciting journey she'd ever experienced by being trapped in the hold. She was at sea again! That part was like a dream come true. She scratched Spike behind his ears thoughtfully.

Marina pulled out a small dagger she'd hidden in her clothes. She wriggled the blade into the crack of the door. A moment later she'd loosened the pin from one of the hinges. She smiled as she heard it hit the floor.

The door swung open and Marina stepped out onto the deck. She glanced back at Spike. "Oh, come on. You look great," she said, then glanced around at the crew. Spike reluctantly stepped into the daylight, ribbons tied around his ears in big floppy bows.

"Look lively!" Kale shouted from nearby. "Jed! Get the longpoles!"

A line swung toward her, and she ducked to avoid it. She

turned around just in time to jump out of another sailor's way as he rushed past.

"Pardon me, m'lady," he called over his shoulder.

Marina glanced around, wondering what was going on. As soon as she noticed where they were heading, she understood. Jutting out of the water were dozens of huge, jagged towers of rock.

"The Dragon's Teeth," she murmured in awe.

A voice responded from directly above her. "Indeed, *signorina*." Glancing up, Marina saw a skinny little sailor hanging from a line. "Only the most foolish of captains would dare to sail a ship through—"

"Rat!" Sinbad interrupted from somewhere nearby.

As Rat hurried off, Marina followed the sound of Sinbad's voice. He was at the wheel. Didn't he realize how dangerous it was to try to sail through the Dragon's Teeth? Everyone in the Twelve Cities knew the tales of the ships that had disappeared there.

"Are you sure you—" she began.

He cut her off. "Yes, we've done this kind of thing before."

"Look—" Marina said.

"No," he interrupted again. "There is no other way."

"But—" She was getting annoyed. Wasn't he even going to let her finish a sentence?

"And yes," he broke in yet again. "You have my permission to stand there quietly and get a free lesson in sailing."

Marina clenched her fists. He was so infuriating! She was ready to tell him exactly what she thought of him and his free sailing lesson.

But he spoke again before she could find the words. "Besides," he said smugly. "A ship is no place for a woman."

She groaned. Why waste her breath? He was hopeless.

The *Chimera* sailed on. Soon the tall, eerie rocks of the Dragon's Teeth surrounded it on all sides. The ship slowly glided through the water. Nobody wasted any words as the crew navigated around the deadly rocks.

"Steady as she goes," Sinbad told his men.

Wisps of fog danced across the deck. Marina held her breath as the ship just missed some submerged rocks. One of the men pointed silently to something ahead. When she looked through the ghostly fog, she saw the wreckage of a ship half hidden in the water. She shuddered.

"Steady," Sinbad murmured as the crew guided the *Chimera* beneath the ravaged prow of one of the wrecks. Water dripped onto the deck from the face of the broken ship's figurehead, the carved wooden woman at the prow.

Just then Marina heard a noise. It was faint at first, but soon grew louder. Voices? She strained to listen. It was unlike anything she'd heard before.

"What is that sound?" she asked.

Marina glanced over at Sinbad. His expression was distant and slightly dazed. Was he listening, too? The sound grew

louder, blending into a haunting, hypnotic song.

She peered into the fog. The figurehead of the sunken ship they'd passed came to life as a watery, ghostlike figure, slipping into the sea. On another wreck, another figurehead came to life and dropped into the water.

At the rail, Spike began to bark. Marina hurried to him and looked over the side. The shapes were swimming after the *Chimera*, their haunting song rising up around the ship. She gulped as she realized what they were.

Sirens! The bewitching sea spirits who lured men to watery graves with their eerie song.

She raced back to the wheel. "Sinbad?" She shook him, but he didn't respond.

Crack!

Marina nearly fell as the ship smashed against a rock.

Glancing around in a panic, Marina saw that the other men had abandoned their posts. They were wandering around the deck in a daze, spellbound by the Sirens' song.

The ship was heading straight toward a huge outcropping. Shoving Sinbad aside, Marina grabbed the wheel. Spike whined anxiously as she managed to steer past the rocks. Whew! That had been close.

But the Sirens weren't through with them yet. They rose up in front of the ship like a tidal wave. Laughing, singing, and calling, they beckoned the entranced crew toward the water. The men staggered toward them.

Marina glanced around wildly. What could she do? If she left the wheel, the ship would smash against the rocks. But if she didn't, the men would follow the Sirens straight off the edge of the deck.

Spike whined anxiously again. That gave Marina an idea.

She grabbed a rope and put it between the dog's teeth. "Round the deck," she told him. "Now!"

Spike wagged his tail and took off. He raced around the crewmen, looping the rope around them and yanking them back into the middle of the deck.

The Sirens wailed angrily. One of them called to Rat. He leaped from his perch in the crow's nest, landing in the water with a splash.

"Mi amore!" he called to the Siren. "I love you!"

Feeling desperate, Marina looked at Sinbad lying on the

deck in a daze. She pulled him upright and propped him against the wheel to hold it steady. Then she grabbed a hook and rope, threw it over the yardarm, and swung it out over the water.

She managed to hook the drowning Rat by his pants. She swung back to the deck and started hauling Rat back onboard. Suddenly, she noticed that one of the Sirens had lured Sinbad away from the wheel! He staggered toward the edge of the deck.

Marina couldn't let go of the rope or she would lose Rat. But she had to save Sinbad. "Spike!" she hollered. "Get Sinbad!"

The dog leaped forward. Sinbad yelped as Spike bit down on the seat of his pants.

Marina dragged Rat onto the deck and raced back to the

wheel. With no one steering, the *Chimera* was heading straight toward the wreck of another ship. Jagged peaks of rock rose on either side—there was nowhere to go.

Taking a deep breath, she held the wheel steady, aiming straight toward the wreckage. "Spike!" she called. "The blades!"

Proteus had mentioned the *Chimera*'s special feature when recounting the battle with Eris's sea monster. With the pull of a lever, metal blades shot out of the sides, slicing through anything that got in their way.

Now, they cut easily through the wrecked ship. The Sirens howled in anger and frustration as the *Chimera* sailed through the obstacle and landed with a tremendous splash in the calm waters of the open sea.

CHAPTER FIVE
A Strange Island

It was a few minutes before the crew were themselves again. Meanwhile Marina stood at the wheel and kept the ship on course. After steering through the Sirens and the Dragon's Teeth, the open sea was downright easy. Marina felt proud of what she had just done. She had saved the ship and the crew. That should make Sinbad think twice about insulting her again.

Eventually the men came out of their daze and started wandering around, trying to figure out what had happened. "Sinbad saved us," one of them said groggily.

"No, Marina!" Rat corrected.

"Marina saved us," the other men muttered. "Marina? Marina!"

Sinbad walked toward her. Spike wagged his tail and led the way.

Marina bent down with a smile as Spike bounced toward her. "Hey, if it isn't my little hero." She greeted him fondly with a pat. "You were so brave! What a good dog!"

Sinbad scratched his head. "Uh . . ." he began.

Marina turned toward him with a smile. "Still think a ship's no place for a woman?"

He hesitated. "Absolutely," he responded after a moment. He gestured around him. "I mean, look at my ship!"

She stared at him in disbelief.

"This railing is hand-carved mahogany," he complained, pointing at a damaged part of the staircase. "And these moldings came all the way from Damascus. Do you have any idea what I went through to steal these?" He turned to frown at her. "This is exactly why women shouldn't drive!"

"Are you crazy?" Marina exclaimed. "I saved your life!"

"Oh, I would have been fine. I always am." With that, he pushed her aside and took her place at the wheel.

Marina couldn't believe it. He still refused to admit that he had been wrong about her! She stomped away to her "cabin" in disgust. The crew watched her sympathetically.

A few minutes later, someone pounded on the door. She

flung it open and found Sinbad standing there.

"What?" Marina demanded, still annoyed.

"Thank you!" he shouted.

"You're welcome!" she retorted.

"No problem!"

"Don't worry about it!"

"I won't!"

"Good!"

"Good-bye!"

"Bye to you!"

With that, she slammed the door shut again. She blinked in surprise. Then she smiled.

Maybe Proteus hadn't been crazy to call Sinbad his friend. In fact, maybe there was hope for him after all. At least a little.

Later, the ship dropped anchor off a very strange-looking island to take care of repairs. Sinbad was still complaining about all the damage. Marina walked by as he was muttering about the stair railing again. For such a big strong man, she thought, he certainly could act like a baby.

"Oh, for heaven's sake," she told him. "You only need a little tree sap and she'll be as good as new."

She grabbed a bucket and headed down the gangplank with Spike trotting happily behind her. Maybe if she found the sap, Sinbad would stop his whining. The rest of the crew members were quick to offer their help as she stepped off the ship.

"Why, thank you," she told them. "How nice to see some men haven't forgotten common courtesy."

Marina had never seen an island quite like this. The ground was covered with odd-looking plants and large flat rocks. In the center of the island was a large round mountain, but no plants grew there.

Sinbad caught up with her as she headed for a promising-looking tree trunk. "I already said thank you," he said. "That's what this is all about, isn't it?"

"It's about repairing the ship," Marina told him calmly. "If I break something, I fix it." She peered at the trunk and stuck out her hand. "Knife, please."

"Oh, yeah." Sinbad snorted. "Like I'd give you a weapon."

The rest of the crewmen were still following them. Immediately, each of the men offered whatever knife, sword, or other blade he had at hand. Marina selected one.

"Thank you, Rat," she told the blade's owner. Then she smiled sweetly at Sinbad.

She sliced into the tree trunk as the men—except for Sinbad—chatted happily about how she was going to fix the ship. Oddly enough, the tree shuddered slightly. But sap poured out into her bucket. Soon it was full.

"This girl wouldn't know how to fix a broken fingernail," Sinbad commented to the crew as Marina turned around.

"Honestly!" she snapped as she walked toward him with the sap bucket. She was fed up with his bad attitude. "You are the most boorish, pigheaded man I've ever met!"

He muttered something as he turned and walked away. Marina was doing her best to be mature, but this was too much!

She let the bucket of sap fly. *Wham!* It hit him square in the back of the head. The sap slopped out all over him. The rest of the crew gasped in shock as Sinbad turned slowly to face her.

Marina stared back at him. He grabbed a handful of gloppy sap.

"Oh no," Marina said, suddenly regretting her impulsive act. "Oh ho ho, no!"

Sploosh! A second later she had a faceful of sap.

She brushed it away, moving in on him. "You egotistical, selfish . . ."

He held his ground. "You spoiled . . ."

"Disrespectful, pretentious . . ."

"Deluded . . ."

Marina grabbed a large, crablike thing from the ground. She wasn't even sure what it was. But she lobbed it furiously at Sinbad's head.

He dodged. She tried again. This time whatever-it-was connected with his jaw.

"Untrustworthy, ungrateful," Marina cried, grabbing for a rock on the ground. "Impossible, insufferable ... "

The rock was heavier than it looked. At first it wouldn't budge. Then she yanked it free, holding it over her head.

Before she could take aim, a tremor ran through the ground beneath their feet. Marina, Sinbad, and the crew all stared curiously at the rock in her hands.

"Put it back," Sinbad said urgently.

Marina laughed nervously, not sure whether to argue or do as he said. Suddenly, in the water behind them, a giant fish tail emerged with a tremendous splash. The "mountain" in the center of the island was making a strange gurgling sound. Marina finally realized what was happening as a giant eye opened in the ground beneath her feet. This wasn't an island at all. It was an enormous fish!

Sinbad and the rest of the crew had just recognized the same thing. "Run!" Sinbad shouted. "Come on!"

They all raced toward the ship as the creature beneath them heaved and shuddered. The ground suddenly fell away right in front of them. It was the creature's huge gill opening.

Sinbad grabbed Marina's arm and leaped across the

gill. They barely made it. The rest of the crew followed. They all slip-slided toward the ship.

Somehow they scrambled aboard. Sinbad grabbed a rope to swing himself and Marina up to the top deck. Then he scrambled toward the stern, scooping up a rope and hook as he went. He tossed the loose end to Rat.

"Tie this off!" he called.

"Wh—what?" Rat stammered in surprise.

Without bothering to respond, Sinbad heaved the hook back toward the giant island-fish. It skittered across the creature's back, finally lodging in its rocky scales.

"Ha!" Sinbad cried in triumph.

Marina gulped, realizing what he was doing as the rope snapped tight. The big fish "island" was towing the ship!

The *Chimera* rocketed forward as the giant fish took off at top speed.

CHAPTER SIX
The Roc

The ship made great progress. However, being dragged along by a giant, annoyed fish didn't make for the smoothest ride. Before long, the entire crew was seasick. Even Spike.

"Sinbad," Kale panted. "The men can't take much more."

Sinbad was doubled over at the side of the ship. "I can't take much more, either," he said. "Cut the line."

Kale did as he said, and the ship slowed immediately. Marina staggered toward Sinbad, who was still leaning over the rail.

"Whose idea was that again?" Sinbad joked weakly.

"I don't know," Marina responded, "but he owes me lunch."

They exchanged a look that was almost a smile. It was funny how almost getting killed could make things a little friendlier.

Then Sinbad gestured at the view ahead. Marina looked and noticed two massive stone gates on the horizon.

"The Granite Gates," he said. "Bet you never thought I'd get us this far."

"No, I didn't," she replied honestly. "But Proteus did. For some reason, he trusts you."

"What could he have been thinking?" Sinbad quipped.

Marina had been wondering the same thing for a while now. "How did you two ever meet?" she asked curiously.

Sinbad shrugged. "I was running for my life, as usual." He glanced over at her. For a moment she thought that was all he was going to say. Then he continued. "A couple of angry thugs had cornered me outside the palace walls. I was trapped. And then suddenly, there was Proteus. He had watched it all from his room in the palace. He had actually climbed down the castle wall to fight at my side. We were best friends from that day forward."

Marina smiled. That sounded just like Proteus. "What happened with you two?"

Sinbad looked uncomfortable. "We took different paths," he said. Then he turned away.

Before Marina could ask more questions, she noticed a chill in the air. The ship wasn't moving. The sea around the *Chimera* had begun to freeze. The boat was trapped in the ice.

The men did their best to break the ice and keep the ship moving. Some of them hopped overboard, hacking at the hard icy surface.

Suddenly Spike began to bark. Marina spotted something in the distance high above some snowy cliffs. It flew closer, let out a loud shriek, then disappeared.

The shape emerged again, crashing over the icy cliffs. It appeared to be a gigantic bird of prey with huge talons and a deadly-looking beak.

It was the Roc, another of Eris's monsters. "Everyone back on the ship!" Sinbad shouted as the creature swooped toward the *Chimera*.

The next few moments passed in chaos and confusion. The Roc circled and dove as the sailors skittered across the ice. Finally all were safe aboard the ship except for Jed.

The Roc plummeted directly toward the helpless man. Just as the creature's talons reached for him, Jed dove into the icy water near the ship. As the Roc banked and circled, Marina peered over the edge of the ship. Jed surfaced, gulping for air.

"Jed!" Marina called. "Grab the rope!"

She tossed a rope overboard. Just as she was dragging Jed over the railing, she heard Sinbad shouting her name. As she glanced over her shoulder, a huge shadow fell over her. She looked up and saw the Roc diving straight toward her.

Marina tried to run, but it was too late. The Roc grabbed

her in its talons and lifted her off the deck. Sinbad dove for her and grabbed her hand. She tried to hold on to him, but the Roc was too strong. Sinbad lost his grip and fell away as the Roc carried Marina toward the sky.

The Roc dropped her into its nest high atop a tower of ice. It shrieked loudly as it came in for a landing nearby.

Marina tried to escape. But there was nowhere to go. Everywhere she turned, the Roc was there, holding her like a prisoner under its talons. Finally she was able to wriggle free and dive beneath a giant rib cage—the remains of the Roc's last meal, she guessed.

The Roc screeched as it looked for her. Marina held her breath, pressing herself against the bones. Would it figure out where she was?

And even if it didn't, what would happen next? She was in big trouble. And for once, she wasn't sure how she was going to get out of it.

A few minutes passed without a sound from the Roc. Marina peeked out to see what it was doing. As she did, a hand clamped over her mouth.

She let out a startled shout that was only partly muffled by the hand. The Roc turned toward her and shrieked.

"Shh!" Sinbad hissed behind her.

Marina pushed his hand away, then turned to him in

amazement. "You're rescuing me!" she whispered. Again, she spied a decent man beneath the swaggering, annoying exterior.

"Yes," Sinbad whispered back. "If that's what you want to call it. But this is going to cost you another diamond. Rescues aren't part of the usual tourist package."

She should have known. "So," she said. "How are we going to get down?"

Sinbad glanced around thoughtfully. "I don't know yet."

"What?" Marina whispered angrily.

Sinbad clapped his hand over her mouth again. "I'm thinking about it, all right?"

She pulled his hand away. "You scaled a thousand-foot tower of ice and you don't know how to get down?"

"Of all the ungrateful—" he began. "Look, if you'd rather take chances on your own, that can be arranged."

Just then Marina heard a squawk from outside the rib cage. The Roc was moving closer. "Shh," she hushed Sinbad. They were in this together now. She decided she might as well try to look on the bright side. "All right, all right. So what do we have to work with? Ropes?"

Sinbad looked sheepish. "No."

"Grappling hooks?"

"Yeah—no," he admitted.

This was looking worse by the second. He was holding a shield, but otherwise his hands were empty. Hadn't he thought this through at all? "Your swords?" Marina asked hopefully.

Sinbad's expression brightened. He pulled out a dagger. "I've got this!"

"Great," Marina muttered. "He can pick his teeth when he's done with us."

"In the hands of an expert, a good knife has a thousand and one uses," Sinbad said. He spun the dagger and flipped it. It hit the ice overhead.

CRASH!

Their hiding place collapsed around them. The Roc turned and spotted them immediately.

Sinbad grabbed Marina. "Come on!" he said, dragging her toward the cliff's edge.

"What?" she protested as they teetered there for a second. Glancing down, she spotted the *Chimera* in the ocean far, far below. It looked very small and far away.

Sinbad pulled her over the drop-off. "Let's goooooo!"

CHAPTER SEVEN
An Icy Ride

"Nooo!" Marina cried as she and Sinbad fell, and fell, and fell down the ice tower.

Sinbad pulled his shield underneath the two of them. Soon they were flying down the steep slope on the makeshift sled.

"I think we lost him," Sinbad said breathlessly as they skidded between giant columns of ice.

There was a loud, angry shriek from directly overhead.

"I don't think so," Marina replied grimly.

The Roc swooped overhead and dove again. Still they slid faster and faster. Marina could see the *Chimera* in the water far below. Would they make it? She wasn't too sure of that.

The Roc dove at them again and again. The giant bird hit a column and sent it crashing into its neighbor. Suddenly the huge columns were coming down in front of Sinbad and Marina like dominoes. Marina struggled to hold on as they careened inside the tower. It was too fast. The columns were too close!

Huge chunks of ice flew at them as they dodged left and right. Sinbad spotted an opening in the ice tower, and leaned hard to turn the sled. But the Roc smashed through the wall, shattering it into icicles.

The Roc was still behind them, and was closing in. It shrieked and dove. Sinbad stood on the moving sled like a snowboard and pulled Marina to her feet. They leaned left and right, skittering over the shards of ice inside the tower. But Sinbad kept the sled on course, dodging the flying ice and snow as well as the Roc's talons. Suddenly, Sinbad spotted a ray of sunlight through a narrow opening in the ice wall.

"Hang on!" Sinbad yelled.

Before Marina could protest, he planted his dagger in the ice and spun the sled out over the cliff. The two of them hung in the air for what seemed like forever, before tumbling down the giant slope. Luckily, they landed in the soft canvas of the *Chimera*'s sails, far below.

"There," Sinbad said breathlessly. "Just as I planned."

Marina stared at him. Then she laughed. Sinbad might be crazy, but she had to admit that he knew how to get things done. He grinned back at her.

The crew raced over to untangle them. "It's Marina!" the men cried happily. Someone helped her to her feet. Rat rushed forward to hug her.

"Oh, I'm fine," Sinbad said wryly. "But I'm touched by your concern."

He grimaced as he stood and his back let out a loud crack of protest.

From somewhere nearby, there was another crack. Then a rumble and crash.

They all looked around and saw the ice tower falling into the sea. The frozen surface shattered, and a wide waterway opened up before them. The ship was free.

The *Chimera* sailed on through the night, following Eris's star. As Marina wandered around the deck, she saw Sinbad at the wheel.

She walked over to join him. There was something she had to say.

"Sinbad," she told him hesitantly. "Thank you for coming after me."

He turned with a smile. For a moment Marina thought he was going to crack a joke. Instead, he simply said, "You're welcome."

He turned back to his task. Marina watched him for a moment. He seemed relaxed and at home there at the wheel, watching the ocean glide by.

"This life suits you," she told him sincerely.

"I wasn't made for dry land." He glanced at her. "And you? Is it the shore or the sea?"

"I've always loved the sea," she admitted. "I even dreamed of a life on it. But it wasn't meant to be."

Sinbad was silent for a moment. Then he took her hand and placed it on the wheel. "You know," he said, "I've traveled the world. Seen things no other man has seen. But nothing compares to the open sea."

They stood there together, looking out over the waves. And for the first time, Marina felt they understood each other, at least a little.

For the first time, it felt as though they were friends.

A few minutes later there was a crash of thunder. A flash of light cut through the night sky. A shooting star.

There was another flash. Sinbad frowned.

"The gates of Tartarus," he said.

Marina looked forward. Eris's star was hanging in their path, seeming to touch the waves. Everyone stared in amazement at what lay before them. Eris's star was really an enormous gateway in the night sky. Rat scurried up to the crow's nest and reported that they were approaching the edge of the world. The gateway to Tartarus lay just beyond, floating in the dark sky just beyond the edge of the ocean.

Marina glanced at Sinbad uneasily. Now what?

"Men!" Sinbad ordered suddenly. "All hands to your posts. Free all sheets and wait for my command."

The men stared at him. Marina could tell they were

wondering if he'd gone crazy. She was wondering the same thing.

"Now!" Sinbad shouted. "Go! Go! Go!"

Sinbad continued to shout orders. Marina had no idea what he was trying to do. But there was no time. They just had to trust him. She swung into action along with the others, following Sinbad's instructions.

Finally the sails were positioned as ordered. "Pull!" he shouted.

The crew strained at the ropes. The sails billowed. The *Chimera* sailed closer and closer to the edge. The men tied off the sails and waited.

The ship teetered at the edge of the ocean. Everyone braced themselves. The prow tipped over the edge. The rest of the ship followed. It felt as though they were falling off the edge of the Earth.

For a terrifying moment, Marina thought it was all over. Her stomach flipped as she felt the ship drop like a stone.

Then the sails filled in the updraft. The ship bobbled and lifted up! It floated there in the air beyond the edge of the Earth.

"It worked!" Sinbad murmured to Marina. He sounded relieved.

Cheers rose from the other crew members. Marina just smiled in amazement and relief as the *Chimera* flew across the abyss toward the gateway.

Sinbad stared into it. Then he turned. "Hard over to port,

Grum," he called to one of the men.

The ship turned. Sinbad called Kale forward.

"If I don't make it," he told him, "the ship is yours." He saluted the rest of the crew. "Gentlemen, it's been a privilege robbing with you."

Marina understood immediately. Sinbad wasn't going to risk his crew's life. He was planning to go into Tartarus alone.

She stepped forward. "I'm coming with you."

Sinbad started to say something. But she cut him off.

"And don't tell me the realm of Chaos is no place for a woman," she warned.

Sinbad pulled her toward him. He wrapped a rope around her waist, then around himself.

"I would never say that," he told her.

Marina smiled. She held on as Sinbad jumped over the rail and swung them toward the arched gateway.

CHAPTER EIGHT

The Realm of Chaos

Marina and Sinbad floated through the air until suddenly they were standing. Just standing. A bleak, empty landscape of swirling sand surrounded them.

Tartarus.

The sands parted and revealed a horde of celestial monsters. They encircled Sinbad and Marina. Sinbad pulled out his sword as the creatures moved closer.

"Now, now, my pets," a female voice purred from the shadows. "Is this any way to treat a guest?"

The sands instantly revealed a pair of ordinary chairs. They looked very out of place in that strange world.

A moment later Eris herself appeared. "Bravo," she said. "No mortal has ever made it to Tartarus before. Alive, that is. Make yourselves at home."

"Nice place you've got here," Sinbad commented dryly.

"Like it?" Eris cooed. "I'm planning on doing the whole world this way."

"I see you're busy," Sinbad said. "So listen, we'll just take the Book of Peace and get out of your way."

But Eris wasn't about to let the Book go that easily. "What makes you think I have it?"

"Well, you framed me for the theft so they would execute me," Sinbad said. Eris smirked. He suddenly realized his mistake. "No, Proteus!" he cried. "You knew he would take my place!"

"What a clever little man you are," Eris cooed.

"You thought I'd run," Sinbad went on. "Then Proteus would die and Syracuse would be—"

"Left without the next rightful king," Eris finished for him. "And tumble into glorious chaos! You humans are so predictable. Proteus couldn't help being ever-so-noble and you couldn't help betraying him."

"But I didn't betray Proteus!" Sinbad protested. "I didn't run away."

"Oh, but you did betray him," Eris said, gesturing at Marina. "You stole his only love! He's not even in his grave yet and you're moving in on his girl! Face it, your heart is as black as mine."

Marina stepped forward. "You don't know what's in his heart," she cried. Hadn't she misjudged him once herself? She had thought him selfish and boorish. But his actions during the voyage had proved to her that his rough exterior covered a heart capable of true friendship.

Eris smiled knowingly at Sinbad. "In your heart you know

that Proteus is going to die because he saw something in you that just isn't there."

"No!" Sinbad cried.

"Want to bet?" Eris replied. "I'll tell you what. Let's play a game. If you win I'll give you the Book of Peace." With a wave of her hand, the Book appeared on a floating platform. "There it is, noble hero."

Sinbad stepped toward the Book. But as he did, part of the platform crumbled beneath his feet.

"Not so fast," Eris said. "My game has rules, Sinbad. I'll ask you one simple question. If you answer truthfully, the Book is yours."

He still looked wary. "Give me your word."

Eris sighed. "You still don't trust me? Oh, all right, you have my word as a goddess." She made a motion over her chest, and a fiery X appeared there. "Fair enough?" she said.

Sinbad turned to stare at the Book. His expression was intense. "Ask your question."

"Now we all know what happens if you get the Book of Peace. You return it to Syracuse and save Proteus. But if you don't get the Book, you have a choice to make. Either sail to paradise with the woman of your dreams, or return to Syracuse to die. You're either a thief, or a hero. So here's my question, Sinbad. If you don't get the Book, will you go back to die?"

There was a long moment of silence. Sinbad looked at Marina. Then he looked at the Book.

"I will go back," he said.

Again, silence. Sinbad reached cautiously toward the Book.

Then the ground cracked beneath him.

"You're lying," Eris hissed.

Marina felt herself hurled out of Tartarus. Sinbad flew through the air beside her. Eris's mocking laughter followed them as they fell.

Return to Syracuse

They landed on a barren strip of sand. Gray waves lapped at the shore. The gateway to Tartarus loomed in the distance.

Marina glanced over at Sinbad. He looked completely hopeless.

"I'm sorry, Marina," he spoke at last. "Eris is right about me."

"No, she's not," she said. "You answered her question. You told the truth."

"It wasn't the truth. It was me, trying to pass myself off as someone I'm not."

Marina hated seeing him look so beaten. "Sinbad, I've seen who you are," she insisted. "You don't need to pretend. Eris trapped you. Why should you or Proteus or anyone have to die?" It just wasn't fair. Why should Sinbad suffer for something Eris had done? "You need to escape," she urged him. "Get as far away as you can. I'll go back. I'll explain everything."

She was sure she could do it. She could convince the others to release Proteus without sacrificing Sinbad in his place. It was the only thing that made sense now that the Book was gone for good.

Sinbad shook his head helplessly. "No, Marina," he began.

She cut him off, knowing what he was going to say. "I can't watch you die!" she cried. "I love you."

Sinbad looked stunned. He held out his hands to her. "But could you love a man who would run away?"

He knew what he had to do.

The *Chimera* arrived back in Syracuse just in time. Proteus was at the block facing his doom when Sinbad, Marina, and the crew rushed in.

"Bet you thought I wouldn't make it," Sinbad said lightly.

Proteus looked relieved. "I was beginning to wonder," he retorted. Then he looked at Sinbad's empty hands and frowned. "The Book?"

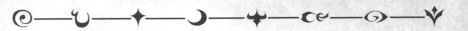

"I did my best," Sinbad said quietly. "But it wasn't enough."

"No," Proteus cried. "You came back anyway?"

"How could I do anything else?" Sinbad replied. "My friend."

Then he turned and kneeled down, taking Proteus's place.

Marina watched from nearby with the crew. She buried her face in Spike's fur, not wanting to see. But she couldn't resist one last look.

The sword came toward Sinbad . . . and exploded into a million fragments.

A cloud suddenly swirled over the city. Shadows twisted together into one huge dark form.

Marina gasped. It was Eris!

The Goddess of Chaos whirled on Sinbad, her eyes blazing.

"How dare you?" she howled in fury. "Everything was going perfectly and now you do this?"

"Wait a minute." Understanding dawned in Sinbad's eyes. "I didn't lie. I came back! That's why you're here. This was all part of your test. I told the truth!"

Eris fumed and clenched her fists. But the glowing X blazed on her chest, proving that Sinbad was right. She had given her word—and Sinbad had passed her test.

Opening her hand, she revealed the Book of Peace. Sinbad

grabbed it. Then Eris vanished in a swirl of darkness. He opened the book, and a burst of light came from the pages. Before their eyes, the light washed the destruction from Syracuse, leaving it gleaming and magical.

Proteus rushed forward. "For what it's worth," he told Sinbad, "I think the council believes you now."

Marina laughed with relief. They had succeeded! And all because Sinbad had followed his heart.

And now she knew it was time to follow her own heart. No more boring ambassador duties for her. She knew Proteus would understand. In fact, she didn't think he would be surprised when she told him. Sinbad had been a good friend to him, and he would be happy that they had come to mean so much to each other.

Marina smiled, thinking about how much her feelings toward Sinbad had changed over the course of their journey together. They had gone from foes to friends, and then something more. She couldn't wait to head back to the open seas in search of more adventures as part of the *Chimera*'s crew, with Sinbad by her side.

THE END

Sinbad: Legend of the Seven Seas
Junior Novelization

Sinbad: Legend of the Seven Seas
8 x 8 Storybook

Sinbad: Legend of the Seven Seas
Adventure Fun Book